I NEED TO
HOPE IN GOD

GOD AND ME

BOOKS IN SERIES

I Need to Trust in God
I Need to Hope in God
I Need to Love God
I Need to Love Other People

I NEED TO HOPE IN GOD

Joel and Mary Beeke

Illustrated by Cassandra Clark

Reformation Heritage Books
Grand Rapids, Michigan

I Need to Hope in God
© 2021 by Joel and Mary Beeke

Reformation Heritage Books
3070 29th St. SE
Grand Rapids, MI 49512
616-977-0889
orders@heritagebooks.org
www.heritagebooks.org

Printed in China
21 22 23 24 25 26/10 9 8 7 6 5 4 3 2 1

Library of Congress Cataloging-in-Publication Data

Names: Beeke, Joel R., 1952– author. | Beeke, Mary, author. | Clark, Cassandra, illustrator.
Title: I need to hope in God / Joel and Mary Beeke ; illustrated by Cassandra Clark.
Description: Grand Rapids, Michigan : Reformation Heritage Books, [2021] | Series: God and me |
    Audience: Ages 4–7
Identifiers: LCCN 2021002922 | ISBN 9781601788702 (hardcover)
Subjects: LCSH: Hope—Religious aspects—Christianity—Juvenile literature.
Classification: LCC BV4638 .B44 2021 | DDC 234/.25—dc23
LC record available at https://lccn.loc.gov/2021002922

For additional Reformed literature, request a free book list from Reformation Heritage Books at the above regular or email address.

MEMORY VERSE

"We are saved by hope" (Romans 8:24).

It was a fun day in the sun. Caleb and Sophie said good-bye to their cousins.

All that good food and outdoor play made their eyelids heavy....

Rain splashed.
Lightning flashed.
Thunder crashed.

"Mommy, the storm is so loud."

"Can you see the road, Daddy?"

TALK ABOUT IT

1. How can the Holy Spirit teach you to hope in Jesus who died for sinners like us?

2. How will your life change by the Holy Spirit when your hope is in Jesus Christ?

Note to parents: Saving, biblical hope is the confident expectation of what God has promised to His people in Jesus Christ; its strength lies in God's faithfulness. Explain to your children that they need a saving hope from the Holy Spirit that looks to Jesus, and God's promises in Him, for everything we need in this life and for the life to come.

"Lord, we thank Thee for bringing us safely home tonight, and
for fulfilling our hopes. Please help us to hope in Jesus, so tha
we know we will be taken care of in this life—even when bad
things happen—and forever. For Jesus's sake. Amen."

"What is hope?"

"Hope is like a safe shelter in a storm. When we hope in God, we trust His promise that He will take care of our soul and body for the sake of Jesus. The Bible says, 'We are saved by hope'" (see Romans 8:24).

"If God gives us a new heart, then, even if scary things happen, we have hope in God, for today and forever."

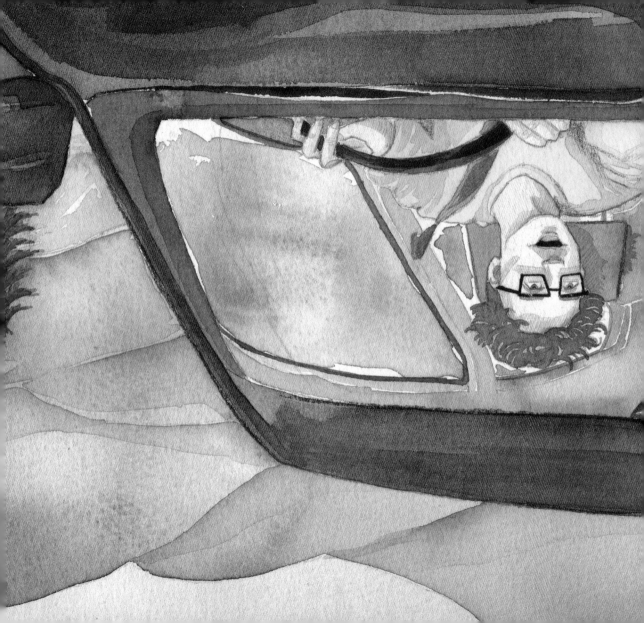

"Yes, God speaks in *all* creation.
And He speaks to us in the Bible."

"Is thunder like God's voice?"